MR. M
at the Park

Roger Hargreaves

Hello, my name is Walter. Can you spot me in this book?

EGMONT

When Mr Bump's alarm went off, he got out of bed, tripped over his slippers, rolled through the door and fell downstairs.

Bump!

Bump!

Bump!

Bump!

And **BUMP!**

And that is the way Mr Bump gets up every morning.

Poor old Mr Bump.

Then the door bell rang.

Mr Bump picked himself up off the floor and went to answer the door.

It was Mr Happy.

"It's a beautiful day," announced Mr Happy. "I think we should have a picnic in the park."

"What a good idea!" cried Mr Bump, tripping over the doormat and squashing Mr Happy.

They packed a hamper and set off for the park and because it was such a lovely day they met lots of their friends on the way who had all had the same idea.

When everyone got to the park they had a delicious picnic.

Just look at the size of Mr Greedy's picnic hamper!

During the picnic a bee kept buzzing round Mr Bump.

He jumped up to wave it away, but he slipped on his sandwich and fell on top of Mr Happy.

After the picnic Mr Happy suggested they hire bicycles.

They all loved their ride round the park.

Just look at Little Miss Magic.

Now, that is magic!

As they were riding past the lake Mr Bump began to wobble and his front wheel bumped the back of Mr Happy's bike.

Which in turn, bumped Mr Happy into…

…the lake.

SPLASH!

When Mr Happy had dried himself off, he suggested they all go boating on the lake.

Everyone had a lovely time rowing round the island.

Just look at Mr Tall.

He does not need a boat!

As they were returning to the bank, Mr Bump, who was rowing, missed a stroke, toppled over backwards and bumped Mr Happy into the lake.

Again!

SPLASH!

After Mr Happy had dried himself off, again, he suggested they all have a go on the swings.

Just look at how high Mr Strong was pushing Little Miss Giggles.

And how fast Mr Strong made the roundabout go round!

Mr Dizzy was even more dizzy than usual.

Mr Bump thought it might be a good idea to take a walk by himself to the top of the hill to avoid any more accidents.

But.

Oh dear, he tripped and rolled all the way back down the hill and…

... bumped Mr Happy into the lake!

SPLASH!

Poor Mr Happy.

And poor Mr Bump, he felt terrible.

"I'm so sorry," he said.

"I know what we should do next," grinned Mr Happy. "We should ALL go swimming!"

And he pulled Mr Bump into the lake.

SPLASH!

And all the others jumped after him.

SPLASH!

SPLASH!

SPLASH!

And…

SPLASH!

That last splash was Mr Greedy!